800 ANIMAL JOKES FOR KIDS

YOU QUACK ME UP

Q: Why is it dangerous to tell a duck jokes?

A: It might quack up.

An Imprint of Thomas Nelson

You Quack Me Up: 800 Animal Jokes for Kids

© 2025 Tommy Nelson

Tommy Nelson, PO Box 141000, Nashville, TN 37214

Portions of the text were originally published in *JOKE-tionary Jokes*, *LOL-apalooza Jokes*, and *Super-Funny ROFL Jokes* (© 2019 by Thomas Nelson).

All rights reserved. No portion of this book may be reproduced, stored in a retrieval system, or transmitted in any form or by any means—electronic, mechanical, photocopy, recording, scanning, or other—except for brief quotations in critical reviews or articles, without the prior written permission of the publisher.

Published in Nashville, Tennessee, by Tommy Nelson. Tommy Nelson is an imprint of Thomas Nelson. Thomas Nelson is a registered trademark of HarperCollins Christian Publishing, Inc.

Tommy Nelson titles may be purchased in bulk for educational, business, fundraising, or sales promotional use. For information, please e-mail SpecialMarkets@ThomasNelson.com.

ISBN 978-1-4002-5162-9 (eBook)
ISBN 978-1-4002-5160-5 (TP)

Library of Congress Cataloging-in-Publication Data

Names: Brown, Steve, 1977- illustrator.
Title: You quack me up: 800 animal jokes for kids / illustrated by Steve Brown.
Description: Nashville, TN: Thomas Nelson, 2025. | Audience: Ages 5-11 | Summary: "Crack up at more than 800 funny jokes for kids about animals, pets, dinosaurs, birds, and bugs. Your friends and family will laugh out loud at these hilarious questions and answers, knock-knocks, riddles, tongue twisters, and puns"— Provided by publisher.
Identifiers: LCCN 2024054088 (print) | LCCN 2024054089 (ebook) | ISBN 9781400251605 (paperback) | ISBN 9781400251629 (epub)
Subjects: LCSH: Animals—Juvenile humor. | Wit and humor, Juvenile. | LCGFT: Humor.
Classification: LCC PN6231.A5 Y68 2025 (print) | LCC PN6231.A5 (ebook) | DDC 398/.7—dc23/eng/20250101
LC record available at https://lccn.loc.gov/2024054088
LC ebook record available at https://lccn.loc.gov/2024054089

Illustrated by Steve Brown

Printed in the United States

25 26 27 28 29 CWR 10 9 8 7 6 5 4 3 2 1

Mfr: CWR / Robbinsville, NJ / April 2025 / PO #12305085

Contents

The Wacky Wild 1

Pawsitively Pets 37

Birds, Bats, and Buzz 71

Roar, Roar, Dinosaurs! 99

On the Funny Farm 115

Toadily Terrific Reptiles

    and Amphibians 153

Shellebrate Sea Life 171

You Can Write Jokes Too! 195

THE WACKY WILD

How do beavers surf the web?

They just log on.

Why did the beaver eat the light bulb?

It wanted a light snack.

What do you call a pack of bears without ears?

A pack of b.

What do you call a bear in a rainstorm?

A drizzly bear.

How do you cool down a bear's cave in summer?

With a bear conditioner.

A polar bear went into a shop and asked, "Can I please have a . . . . drink?" The shop assistant replied, "Why the

big paws?"

What do you call a bear that has lost all its teeth?

A gummy bear.

What is the best way to talk to a grizzly bear?

From very far away.

Why did the grizzly go to the shoe store?

She was tired of having bear feet.

What happens when a bear falls into a river?

He gets wet.

There once was a young panda bear
Who said, "It's really not fair!
I eat dinner each night
With a tummy so white,
You can see all the food I drop there!"

How does a polar bear build a house without a hammer?

Igloos it together.

Why did everyone at the disco laugh at the panda?

She could bearly dance!

What is the scariest thing pandas eat?

BamBOO!

What did the buffalo say to its kid
that was leaving for college?

"Bison!"

How does a cool camel say hello?

"How you dune?"

Why do camels blend into their environment?

They are camel-flaged.

The cheetah was accused of not telling the truth, so it
said, "Truly, I'm not **lion**!"

There once was a cheetah named Bill
Who suddenly felt rather ill.
It had eaten a bunny
To make it more runny,
But now needs a tummy-fixing pill.

What did the judge say to the cheetah?

"You have a spotty record!"

Why are cheetahs terrible at hide-and-seek?

They're always spotted!

What animal loves potato chips the most?

The chipmunk.

What do you call a deer with no eyes?

I have no eye-deer!

What does the buck say when its
wife asks for something?

"Yes, deer."

Why did the farmer sell the baby deer?

**He needed to earn
a little doe.**

An Australian echidna named Sam
Said, "Birthday parties are my jam!"
But when Sam spun around,
The balloons on the ground
Got hit by its quills and went **bam!**

Why are elephants terrible dancers?

**Because they have
two left feet!**

What do you call an elephant in a phone booth?

A stuck elephant.

What has six legs and a trunk
and lives underground?

An elephant.

The jungle lawyer put forward some evidence, but
the judge said, "That's irr-elephant!"

What did the elephant say to its spouse?

"I love you a ton."

What do foot doctors need to help elephants?

Toe trucks.

An elephant got out of bed
And knocked down a tree with its head.
A meerkat went flying.
A tiger came crying.
"I'm really quite clumsy," it said.

Why wouldn't the elephant work on a computer?

He was afraid of the mouse.

What is gray on the inside but yellow on the outside?

A school bus full of elephants.

What do you call an elephant that hates taking baths?

A smellyphant.

How can you tell when an elephant
is getting ready to charge?

It doesn't have any cash.

How do you know elephants love swimming?

**They always have
their trunks.**

What time is it when ten elephants run past you?

Ten past one.

What vegetable do elephants love?

Squash!

Why did the farmer send an elephant
into his potato fields?

**He wanted mashed
potatoes.**

What do you call a whole bunch of giraffes trying to fit between two trees?

A giraffe-ic jam!

What do you call a giraffe with no eyes?

Graffe.

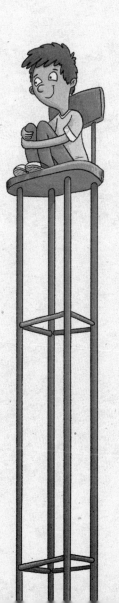

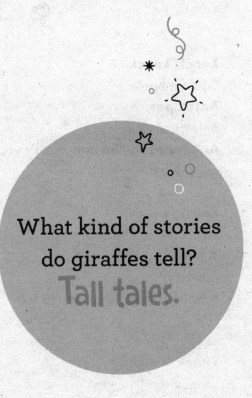

What kind of stories do giraffes tell?

Tall tales.

Knock, knock.
Who's there?
Antelopes.
Antelopes who?
Antelopes so she can marry your uncle.

Knock, knock.
Who's there?
A herd.
A herd who?
A herd this is the place to be!

Knock, knock.
Who's there?
Kanga.
Kanga who?
No, silly, it's kangaroo!

What kind of music did the kangaroos dance to?

Hip-hop.

What do you get when you cross an
elephant and a kangaroo?

Huge holes in the ground all over Australia.

What do you call a lazy baby kangaroo?

A pouch potato.

What looks a lot like half a kangaroo?

The other half of the kangaroo.

A poor little joey cried, "Ouch!"
When it jumped in its mom's warm pouch.
There was no room to share—
An echidna was there,
And it was quite the prickly old grouch!

What animal can put people to sleep?

A hypnopotamus.

What wild animal jumps on one leg?

A hoppopotamus.

What do wild animals sing on your birthday?

Hippo bird-day to you!

What type of hippo always thinks it's sick?

A hippochondriac.

What do you call a laughing hippo?

A happypotamus.

Knock, knock.
Who's there?
Lion.
Lion who?
Lion in the sun is nice!

Knock, knock.
Who's there?
Lion.
Lion who?
Lion is bad. You should tell the truth.

Knock, knock.
Who's there?
A-meer.
A-meer who?
A meerkat who can't reach the doorbell!

What do you call a lion with no eyes?

Lon.

Why don't lions eat clowns?

Clowns taste funny.

A lion walked into a club. It said, "Ow!"

What do you call two lions that like eating together?

Taste buds!

How do lions like their steak cooked?

Medium roar!

An eager young meerkat named Ed
Tripped and then fell on his head.
It got a big bump,
Which turned into a lump,
But it said, "I'm glad I'm not dead!"

What do you call an exploding ape?

A bab**boom!**

What is an ape's favorite dessert topping?

Chocolate chimps.

How can you tell an ape from a mouse?

Pick it up. If it
feels heavy, it's
probably an ape.

What is as big as an ape but doesn't weigh anything?

An ape's shadow.

What is a chimpanzee's favorite Christmas carol?

"Jungle Bells."

Why did someone put a picture of
a bird on top of a gorilla?

They were trying to hold
it up with duck ape.

What do you call a monkey that buzzes?

A chimpan-bee.

What do you call a monkey at the beach?

A chimpan-sea.

What do you call a monkey that likes hot drinks?

A chimpan-tea.

What do you call a monkey that
escaped from the zoo?

A chimpan-free.

What do you call a laughing monkey?
A chimpan-hee-hee-hee!

What do you call a place with hundreds of monkeys?
A chimpan-zoo.

What is a gorilla's favorite fruit?
An ape-ricot.

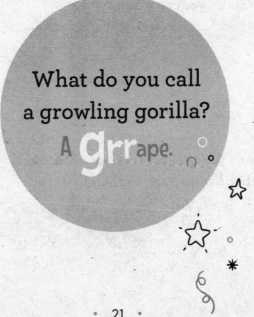

What do you call a growling gorilla?
A grrape.

Knock, knock.
Who's there?
Chimpanzee.
Chimpanzee who?
Chimpanzee unless you poke it in the eye.

What do you call a monkey that wears cool clothes?

A FUNKY MONKEY.

What do you call a monkey that wears cool clothes and has earrings?

A PUNKY, FUNKY MONKEY.

What do you call a monkey that wears cool clothes, has earrings, and fails its exam?

A FLUNKY, PUNKY, FUNKY MONKEY.

> What do you call a monkey that wears cool clothes, has earrings, fails its exam, but is excellent at basketball?

A DUNKY, FLUNKY, PUNKY, FUNKY MONKEY.

> What do you call a monkey that wears cool clothes, has earrings, fails its exam, is excellent at basketball, and smells really bad?

A SKUNKY, DUNKY, FLUNKY, PUNKY, FUNKY MONKEY.

> What do you call a monkey that wears cool clothes, has earrings, fails its exam, is excellent at basketball, smells really bad, and falls in the river?

WET.

Knock, knock.
Who's there?
Joan.
Joan who?
Joan-tcha wanna run? A gorilla's coming!

Knock, knock.
Who's there?
Monkey.
Monkey who?
No, an owl says, "Who." A monkey says, "Oooh-oooh, aaah-aaah!"

What does a proud monkey father call its baby?

A chimp off the old block!

Why did the sick monkey climb into the fridge?

It wanted to feel butter.

What key is terrible at unlocking doors?

The monkey.

Why did the monkey bars move
across the playground?

**They were trying to
get to the other slide.**

Why couldn't the mon get inside?

It forgot its key!

What do you call a monkey with big muscles?

Sir!

What is white and fluffy and swings from cake to cake?

A meringue-utan.

What happens if you don't laugh
at a porcupine's jokes?

It gets a little prickly.

What is the sound of porcupines hugging?
"Ouch!"

Why should you never debate with a porcupine?
You don't want to get their point.

How do you start a reindeer race?
You say, "Ready, set, ho ho ho!"

Knock, knock.
Who's there?
Rhino.
Rhino who?
Rhino you're in there. Let me in!

Why did the girl tie a cord to the rhinoceros?

**She thought it would
be good at charging
her phone.**

What do you call flying skunks?

Smellycopters.

Why did the skunk get a bad grade?

**Its presentation
really stunk.**

Why did the skunks quit four-wheeling?

They kept getting stunk.

Why couldn't the skunk use the restroom?

It was out of odor.

What happens when a skunk publishes a book?

It becomes an instant bestsmeller.

Why was the skunk crying at the movie?

It was really scentimental.

What is black and white and red all over?

A skunk in a tomato fight.

Why did the judge bring a skunk to work?

For odor in the court.

How do you make a skunk stop smelling?

Plug its nose.

Have you heard the skunk joke?

It really stinks.

When is it a good idea to bring a pet skunk to school?
When it's show-and-smell!

Why did the skunk cross the road?
Because the other side stinks.

What is an easy way to catch a squirrel?
Climb a tree and act like a nut.

What is wrong with the food squirrels eat?
They're nuts!

What did the squirrel think of its dinner?
That it was nutty.

What is a squirrel dad's favorite kind of joke?

Acorny one.

What flowers do squirrels like the most?

Forget-me-nuts.

Did you hear about the forest romance?

An acorn was nuts about a squirrel.

Who can help squirrels eat healthier?

A nut-ritionist.

Why did the girl squirrel chase the boy squirrel?

She was nuts about him.

What is a squirrel's favorite dessert?

Doughnuts.

Why did the squirrel chew into the house?

It was looking for wallnuts.

What do you call a tiger with no eyes?

Tger.

Why did the tiger eat the tightrope walker?

It likes a balanced diet.

Why do tigers have stripes?

They don't want to get spotted.

Where did the wolf go to try to be a movie star?

Howlywood.

Why do foxes hunt rabbits?

They like fast food.

Why do foxes have winter coats?

Because they would
look silly in sweaters.

What is black and white and red all over?

An embarrassed zebra.

What do you call a zebra at the North Pole?

Lost.

Can you say these tongue twisters?

The dillydallying armadillo's arms
didn't dig down deep enough.

Big brown boars can't bear when
big brown bears roar.

Bears break black bricks bare-handed.

Excited elephants readily weed red weeds.

Grizzly bears glumly gather in the runny drizzle.

Heartbroken hippos harmonize
with heavenly harps.

Clapping kangaroos quickly kick quiet koalas.

Lions like to lick lollipops in the library.

Magic mathematicians turn monkeys into money.

Wolves wet their whiskers to whistle wildly.

Tricky tigers tickle treacherous tarantulas.

Thirty-six sick, sleepy sloths slurped their soup.

The skunk on the stump surely stunk.

Great apes greedily guzzle gloopy green grapes.

PAWSITIVELY PETS

What do you get when you combine
a bird, a dog, and a car?

A flying carpet.

What is the most musical pet to own?

The trumpet.

Why couldn't the animals agree
on what movie to watch?

The dog wanted an
action movie from
Howlywood. the cat
wanted a **meow**stery.
and the duck demanded
a **duck**umentary.

Knock, knock.
Who's there?
Fur.
Fur who?
Fur crying out loud, let me in!

Knock, knock.
Who's there?
Meow.
Meow who?
Meow-t here, but me want in there.

Knock, knock.
Who's there?
Meow.
Meow who?
Meow-traged at you!

Knock, knock.
Who's there?
Puss.
Puss who?
Puss-ibly the coolest cat you know!

Why did the boy give his sister
a cat for her birthday?

He thought it would
whisker away!

What do you call a cat shaped like a stop sign?

An octopuss.

Where do cats write their essays?

On notebook papurr.

What cat delivers Christmas presents?

Santa Claws!

What do you get when you cross a cat with a dolphin?

A **paw**poise.

Why should you call a cat if you get hurt?
It's a great **purr**amedic!

What do cats eat for dessert?
Chocolate mouse.

What type of cat quacks and swims underwater?
A duck-billed platy-puss.

Why are cats good at gymnastics?
They always get a purrfect score!

What medical procedure do you give a kitten?
A CAT scan.

Where do alien cats get their milk?

From flying saucers.

Why don't you like to watch movies with your cat?

Because it keeps hitting paws.

Why did the cat sit on the keyboard?

It was watching the mouse.

What do a cloned cat and a cheating cat have in common?

One is a cat copy, and the other is a copycat.

What do you call a huge mess caused by your kitten?

A catastrophe.

What is something cats have that
no other animal has?

Kittens!

What did the cat say to its baby?

"Are you kitten me?"

What nursery rhyme does every kitten love?

"Three Blind Mice."

What subject do kittens do well in at school?

Meow-sic class.

How do kittens shop?

From catalogs.

A cat that had fur in bright pink
Tumbled and fell in the sink!
The dishes were clean,
But the cat, it would seem,
Got wet and, boy, did it stink!

Why did the cat eat a lemon?

It was a sourpuss.

What breed of cat likes water?

The octopuss.

What has four legs and cuts grass?

A lawn meower.

What has fur, whiskers, a tail, ears like a cat,
and meows like a cat but is not a cat?

A kitten.

What color do kittens like the most?

Purrple.

What dessert do kittens like the most?

Mice cream.

What does a kitten do in the rain?

It gets wet.

What did the kitten say when it fell?

"MeOW!"

What did the doctor give the sick kitten?

A medicine purrscription.

What is worse than a kitten in a tree?

Two kittens in a tree.

What do you call a kitten with one warm paw?

A KITTEN WITH A MITTEN.

What do you call a kitten with one warm paw that lives in England?

A KITTEN WITH A MITTEN IN BRITAIN.

What do you call a kitten with one warm paw that lives in England and is in love?

A SMITTEN KITTEN WITH A MITTEN IN BRITAIN.

> What do you call a kitten with one warm paw that lives in England, is in love, and sees a dog?

A SMITTEN KITTEN WITH A MITTEN IN BRITAIN THAT IS ABOUT TO BE BITTEN.

> What do you call a kitten with one warm paw that lives in England, is in love, sees a dog, and is saved by a family?

HAPPY.

What did the flea say to the mouse?

"You're enor**mouse**!"

Why did the man put cheese up his nose?

To feed his mousetache!

What do you do if your pet mouse
won't stop squeaking?

Oil it.

What's the only kind of shoes mice will wear?

Squeakers.

How do you spell mousetrap with only three letters?

C-A-T.

There once was a mouse who loved cheese
And stole it from people with ease.
But after a week,
The mousie went, "Eek!"
Its mousehole was now a tight squeeze!

Knock, knock.
Who's there?
Dog.
Dog who?
Doggone it, will you let me in?

Knock, knock.
Who's there?
Pooch.
Pooch who?
Pooch your heads together and figure it out!

Patient: Doctor, I keep thinking I'm a dog.
Doctor: How long have you felt this way?
Patient: Since I was just a wee puppy.

What is a dog's favorite frozen treat?

A pupsicle!

Why are dogs good at wrestling?

Because they're so ruff!

What did the dog say to the tree?

"I like your bark!"

Why did the dog eat the computer?

It could smell the Spam!

What do you call a dog that runs around on Mars?

Rover.

What's a dog's favorite fast food?

Hamburgrr.

What do you call a dog that's always making holes?

A DIGGY DOGGY!

What do you call a dog that's always making holes and leaping?

A FROGGY DIGGY DOGGY!

What do you call a dog that is always making holes, leaping, and loves to dance?

A JIGGY FROGGY DIGGY DOGGY!

What do you call a dog that is always making holes, leaping, loves to dance, and has been out in the rain?

A SOGGY JIGGY FROGGY DIGGY DOGGY!

What do you call a dog that is always making holes, leaping, loves to dance, has been out in the rain, and is wearing a toupee?

A WIGGY SOGGY JIGGY FROGGY DIGGY DOGGY!

What do you call a dog that is always making holes, leaping, loves to dance, has been out in the rain, is wearing a toupee, and is running through the house?

IN TROUBLE!

What is a dog's favorite thing to watch?

A dogumentary.

What do you call a list of dogs?

A dogument!

There once was a poodle named Fred
Who twirled on top of his bed.
He got rather dizzy,
His hair went all frizzy,
And his cheeks turned a bright shade of red!

Why did the Florida puppy pitch left-handed?

It was a southpaw.

What do you call a dog with no legs?

It doesn't matter.
It won't come.

What do you call a dog with no
legs at your front door?

Matt.

What do you call a dog with no legs
swimming in your pool?

Bob.

Why did the dog keep getting splinters in its tongue?

It wouldn't stop
eating table scraps.

Why did the dog keep begging for food?

Because things were ruff.

Why did the mom give the dad a dog and a watch?

She heard he was
having a ruff time.

Why did the Dalmatian think it needed medicine?

It kept seeing spots.

What do you do when it is raining
cats and dogs outside?

Try not to step in
a **poodle**.

What does everyone like less than
raining cats and dogs?

Hailing taxis!

What kind of dog loves fire?

A hotdog.

What do you call a dog that sneezes a lot?

Ahchoo-wawa!

What animal makes the sound *ffur-ffur*?

A dog running backward.

What is something that a dog does
and a human steps into?

Pants.

What did the dog say when its friend
failed obedience school?

"Sorry, that's **ruff**."

Why did the detectives finally leave the dog alone?

They realized they'd
been barking up
the wrong tree.

What dog is great at keeping time?

A watchdog.

What do you use to clean a puppy?

Shampoodle.

A dog owner took their dog to the vet. "Please help," the owner said. "My dog is cross-eyed."

The vet picked up the dog and looked at its eyes, ears, and tongue. Then the vet said, "I'm going to have to put it down."

"Just because it's cross-eyed?" cried the owner.

"No," the vet replied, **"because it's heavy!"**

Why are Dalmatians terrible at hide-and-seek?

They're usually spotted.

Which dog always wins races?

The wiener.

What do you get when you cross a German shepherd with a giraffe?

A watchdog for your tree fort.

What do you do when your dog has a fever?

Cover it in mustard. Nothing is better for a hot dog!

What do you call a dog in a garden?

A collieflower.

What do you call a dog on a porch swing?

A rocker spaniel.

Why is the forest like a pack of dogs?

They both have lots of bark.

What music style do dogs love?

Wagtime.

What did the breeder say to the parents
who wanted a dog for their son?

**"Sorry, we don't
do trades!"**

What did the breeder say to the customer
who asked about any dogs going cheap?

**"Sorry, all of ours
go woof."**

Where at the mall do you find a lot of dogs?

**Most of them are in
the barking lot.**

What do you get when you feed
an angry dog ice cream?

A brr-grr.

What kind of dog barks whenever it hears ticking?

A watchdog.

What do you call a
Labrador mixed with
a poodle that can
do magic tricks?

A labra-cadabra-doodle.

Where do you take a sick puppy?

To the dogter.

Where should you never take your dog shopping?

The flea market.

Why did the two goldfish in the
tank stay totally still?

Neither one knew
how to drive it.

What did the goldfish say at its birthday party?

"Tank you for the gifts."

What is the weasel's favorite ride at the fair?

The ferrets wheel.

Where do guinea pigs go on vacation?

Hamsterdam!

Why couldn't the girl find her guinea pig?

It was playing hide and squeak.

Why do guinea pigs make good spies?

They're good at keeping squeakrets.

Knock, knock.
Who's there?
Bunny ears.
Bunny ears who?
Bunny ears everything you say, so be careful!

Knock, knock.
Who's there?
Some bunny.
Some bunny who?
Some bunny who loves you!

Where do bunnies go when they get married?

On their bunnymoon.

What did the bunny say to the carrot?

"It's been nice gnawing you!"

What do you call a row of rabbits backing up?

A receding hareline.

What do you call a rabbit invention?

A harebrained idea.

Did the rabbits win the relay race?

Yes, by a hare.

What do you call a rabbit stuck in a beehive?

A honey bunny.

What do you call a rabbit with the sniffles?

A runny bunny.

What do you call a rabbit that
memorizes this joke book?

A funny bunny.

How do you catch a wild rabbit?

WITH A CARROT.

How do you catch a tame rabbit?

THE TAME WAY.

Why did the rabbit throw a temper tantrum?

It was hopping mad.

How do furry rabbits fly?

In hareplanes.

Why did the bunny rabbit take off its shoes to dance?

It was at a sock hop.

Where did the rabbits go for breakfast?
IHOP.

What is a rabbit's favorite saying?
"Don't worry. Be hoppy!"

What is a rabbit's favorite song?
"Hoppy Birthday!"

Why did the scientist cross a rabbit with an insect?
He wanted to meet
Bugs Bunny!

What is a rabbit's favorite job?
Haredresser.

Why did the rabbit think it could cross the road?

It didn't. It just hopped it could.

What do you get when you cross
a penguin and a parrot?

A walkie-talkie.

Knock, knock.
Who's there?
A parrot.
A parrot who?
A parrot who?

Can you say these tongue twisters?

Clip a calico cat's claws carefully.

Dopey dogs dribble drinks delightfully.

Clumsy cats can't craftily creep.

Jeff's guinea pigs got jolly.

Can quiet cats quickly clap?

When will rabid rabbits run?

Don't feed a ferocious ferret french fries with filthy fingers.

Pleasant, plucky puppies are playful pets.

Glamorous goldfish gleefully grin from gill to gill.

BIRDS, BATS, AND BUZZ

Why did the bald eagle cross the road?

To shop for a new wig!

Why do bald eagles want to be clowns?

Because of the wigs
they get to wear!

Why didn't the hawks make any plans?

They liked to wing it.

Why did the bird stay in its cage all day long?

No one could budgie it!

What kind of bird wears a hard hat?

A crane.

Person 1: "I returned the rest of my birdseed."
Person 2: "Really? Why?"
Person 1: "Because I planted a bunch of it, and not a single bird grew."

What kind of bird is always sad?

A blue jay.

What type of bird is found on many construction sites?

The crane.

How do crows stay with their flock?

Velcrow.

Why did the boy give his sister a bird for a birthday present?

So it woodpecker!

Why are birds terrible pirates?

They sit in the crow's nest all day.

What did the bird say when the cheetah cheated?

"Toucan play at that game!"

Why is it bad if birds get sick?

They can't be tweeted.

What do you call two birds that are in love?

Tweethearts.

Why did the birds fly south for the winter?

The drive was going to take too long.

What do you give a pet bird when it's sick?

Special tweetment.

Why did the bird leave?
It didn't like the way it was being **tweeted.**

Why should you tell these jokes to baby birds?
They're good for a cheep laugh.

How are birds and flies different?
A fly can't bird, but a bird can fly.

Which are the most religious birds in the wild?
Birds of pray.

Where do lots of birds go on their honeymoon?

To the Canary Islands.

Why did the chickadee go to the doctor?

For medical tweetment.

Why does a flamingo stand on one leg?

Because if it lifted its other leg, it would fall.

Why is the Canadian goose such a rude driver?

It keeps honking.

When do hummingbirds hum?

Whenever they forget the words.

Knock, knock.
Who's there?
Owl.
Owl who?
Owl come in if you open up.

Knock, knock.
Who's there?
Owl.
Owl who?
Owl change the joke a little here in a second.

Knock, knock.
Who's there?
Owl says.
Owl says who?
Yup.

What animal goes *tooh-tooh?*

An owl flying backward.

Why couldn't the owl use the computer?

It had just eaten the mouse.

What did the daughter owl say to her mom as she left for college?

"Don't cry! Owl be back."

What is an owl's favorite subject in school?

Owl-gebra.

The owl told a **hoot** of a joke. Then it overheard other birds **robin** it, which made things really **hawk**-ward! It was even tougher to **swallow** when the raven **crowed** about it.

Person 1: "Did you know you could never lose a homing pigeon?"
Person 2: "Really? Why not?"
Person 1: "Because if you lose it, it was just a regular pigeon."

Why did the pelican get mad leaving the restaurant?
It had a big bill!

Where do penguins keep their money?
In snowbanks.

What is black and white and red all over?
A sunburned penguin.

Ostriches can't fly, but a **pelican**!

Why don't seagulls live in the woods?

Because then they would be forest-gulls.

Why were the lost and thirsty explorers sad?

They found toucans but nothing to drink!

Which animal was the first to play major league sports?

The bat.

What flies around the library every night?

Alpha-bats.

Which animal is at every baseball game?

The bat.

Why do bats get fired from their jobs?

They're always just hanging around.

Knock, knock.
Who's there?
Bee.
Bee who?
Don't worry. Bee happy!

Knock, knock.
Who's there?
Honeybee.
Honeybee who?
Honeybee a sweetheart and open the door.

Person 1: "That bee can't seem to make up its mind."
Person 2: "Really? Why?"
Person 1: "Because it's a may-bee."

Why did the man put a hive on his chin?

He wanted to
grow a bee-rd.

What is a bee's favorite hairstyle?

The beehive.

What will sting you before eating your brains?

A zombee.

What is the healthiest bee?

Vitamin bee.

What happened when a bee flew into a bell?

It was a real **hum**dinger.

Why did the bee go on the roller coaster?

To get a real buzz!

Why did the teacher hate working
at the insect school?

**None of the kids
would beehave!**

What is the smelliest insect?

The bumblebee!

What does a bee do when it finds its honey?

**It offers a marriage
proposal!**

What is smarter than a talking parrot?

A spelling bee!

What animal goes *zzub-zzub*?

A bee flying backward.

There once was a thieving gold bee
Who said, "I take all things for me!"
One theft was a fail;
The bee went to jail
And wailed, "Oh, please set me free!"

Who is every bee's favorite astronaut?

Buzz Aldrin.

Which movie character is every bee's favorite?

Buzz Lightyear.

Why do bees have trouble making friends?

They're real buzzybodies.

What did the teacher say to the unruly bees?

"Please start beehaving."

What do bumblebees in love call each other?

Honey.

What did the bee say when it returned from work?

"Honey, I'm home!"

How do you fix a bee's hair?

With its honeycomb.

What is the best way to get bees to school?

A school buzz.

How is a flower like the letter A?

They both have a bee after them!

Where do all the sick bees go?

To the WASPital.

Who rules the insect world?

The monarch butterfly.

Why did the person throw the
computer at a butterfly?

**They were trying
to get it Internet.**

What is the largest moth?

The mammoth.

"Where are you going?" the queen bee asked the
worker bee as it was flying away.

"I can't live here anymore," the bee replied. "It's
un-bee-lievable!"

How are dogs and fleas different?

A dog can have fleas, but
a flea can't have dogs.

What do you call a fly with no wings?

A walk.

Why did the fly fly?

The spider spied her.

What do flies do outside in the winter?

They **fleas** in the cold!

Did you see the kid who put a
lightning bug in her mouth?

Her face lit up
with delight.

Knock, knock.
Who's there?
Amos.
Amos who?
Amosquito is biting me. Please open the door.

What do lightning bugs say to encourage each other?
"You glow!"

How did the ladybug feel when it got
shot out of the tailpipe of a car?
Exhausted.

Should wasps fly in the rain?
Only if they have
their yellow jackets.

How do you get rid of ants?

Tell them to go find uncles.

What do you call an ant sticking out of the ground?

A plant.

What do you call a really old ant?

An antique.

What kind of ant can knock over a person?

An elephant.

There was a person who loved to dance,
So one day they took a chance.
To be able to move
And really groove,
They put lots of ants in their pants!

What do bedbugs do when they fall in love?

They get married innerspring.

What is the English beetle's favorite sport?

Cricket.

What is the worst type of pillar to use when building tall buildings?

A caterpillar.

What do you get when you eat caterpillars?

Butterflies in your stomach.

What can be on the ground and one hundred feet in the air at the same time?

A centipede on its back.

What is worse than a flamingo with a sore foot?

A centipede with sore feet—it's one hundred times worse.

What is worse than a centipede with sore feet?

A turtle with claustrophobia. It can't go home!

Why did the worm go to New York City?

It wanted to eat the Big Apple!

What do you call an insect that loves music?
A humbug.

Person 1: "Did you hear about the praying mantis in my soup last night?"
Person 2: "No. What was it doing there?"
Person 3: "Saying grace."

Person 1: "A snail got mugged by a turtle."
Person 2: "Really? What happened?"
Person 1: "Nobody knows. When the cops interviewed the snail, it said it all happened too fast!"

Why do French people seem to like eating snails?

They're not fond of fast food.

Where do you find giant snails?

Usually at the end of giants' fingers.

What outdoor sport do spiders like best?

Fly-fishing.

What do you call two spiders who just got married?

Newlywebs.

How does a spider test-drive a car?

It takes it for a spin.

Why didn't the spider excel at sports?

Because it spent too much time on the web.

How did eye doctors help a spider's business?

They improved its websight.

Why did the spider ace the computer test?

It was great on the web.

No one else could find the fly, but the tarantula **spider**.

Can you say these tongue twisters?

A big, black bat bit an itty-bitty rat.

The breeze blew the bumblebees backward.

Clever crows count their claws.

Eleven evil eagles swiped at seven eager beagles.

Flappy flamingos fly freely.

Greasy geese grab globs of green glue.

A few flies flew past fast.

A black bat backtracked too fast and broke its back.

Three bees breezily sneezed.

ROAR, ROAR, DINOSAURS!

Knock, knock.
Who's there?
Herbivore.
Herbivore who?
Herbivore him!

Knock, knock.
Who's there?
Velociraptor.
Velociraptor who?
Velociraptor, but I unwrapped her!

Knock, knock.
Who's there?
T. rex.
T. rex who?
T. rex it and I fix it!

Knock, knock.
Who's there?
Dinosaur.
Dinosaur who?
Dinosaur you!

What do you call a sleeping dinosaur?

A dinosnore.

Why did the T. rex need a bandage?

It had a dinosore.

What makes a dino sore?

Kick it in the shins.

What do dinosaurs smell like?

Exstinked.

Why did the mammoth stop on the side of the road?

It was pulled over by the triceracops!

What do you call a T. rex that wears glasses?

A REX IN SPECS.

What do you call a T. rex that wears glasses and is polite?

A REX IN SPECS WHO RESPECTS.

What do you call a T. rex that wears glasses, is polite, and always pays the bill?

A REX IN SPECS WHO RESPECTS AND PAYS CHECKS.

What do you call a T. rex that wears glasses, is polite, and always pays the bill with a credit card?

A REX IN SPECS WHO RESPECTS AND PAYS CHECKS WITH AN AMEX.

What do you call a T. rex that wears glasses, is polite, always pays the bill with a credit card, and likes to flex its muscles?

A SHOW-OFF!

What do triceratops sit on?

Their tricera-bottoms, I think.

What is a blind dinosaur called?

An I-don't-think-it-saurus.

What do you get when you cross a T. rex with a pig?

Jurassic pork.

What do you call a dinosaur that
uses a lot of big words?

A thesaurus.

What do you call it when dinosaurs
play bumper cars?

Tyrannosaurus wrecks.

What number does the T. rex like the best?

Ate.

What was the biggest dinosaur in Canada?

The Torontosaurus.

What do you get when you cross a
stegosaurus and a centipede?

A legosaurus.

What did the dinosaur say to the archaeologist?

"Can you dig it?"

What brand of watch does a dinosaur wear?

Fossil.

How do you know when a dinosaur tells the truth?

There's no bones about it.

How much does a dinosaur fossil weigh?

A skeleton.

What do you call a short dinosaur?

An ankleosaurus.

Which dinosaur is best at keeping a beat?

The raptor.

Which dinosaur is the politest?

The pleaseiosaur.

What did the little dinosaurs say when their
teacher asked who shot a spitball?

"Iguanadon it!"

Which dinosaur should never go into a museum?

T. wrecks.

Why was it hard for the pterodactyl to sleep?

Because of all the
dinosnores!

Dinosaurs invented perfume. Unfortunately that
made them ex-**stinked!**

Why do we always lose when we play
hide-and-seek with the diplodocus?

Because the dinosaur us!

How did cavemen cut wood?

With a dinosaw.

Why were the dinosaurs spinning around so fast?

They were triceratops.

Why was the teacher mad?

Because the dinoswore!

How does a dinosaur say, "I love you"?

It gives you a diplodokiss.

A T. rex was down at the beach
When it cried out with a loud screech.
While putting on cream,
It needed help, it would seem,
To put cream on the spots it couldn't reach!

What do you say when you meet a dinosaur?
"Allosaurus!"

What do you say when a dinosaur leaves?
"Bye-Ceratops!"

What dinosaur is in the Avengers?
Bronto-Thor-us.

What dinosaur loves Halloween?
The **terror**dactyl.

What do you call a dinosaur that loves playing golf?

A tee rex.

Which dinosaur has the itchiest bite?

A flea rex.

What did the pterodactyl say
when it liked something?

"That was ptotally
pterrific!"

A small dino started to cry
And said, with a tear in its eye,
"I took off my hat
So it wouldn't go flat,
But Brontosaurus has hung it too high."

Can you say these tongue twisters?

The tricky T. rex tried to tickle
three terrified triceratops.

An allosaurus always asks for extras.

There's a troubled triceratops in Texas.

The velociraptor read the book
chapter after chapter.

A million megalodons with a trillion teeth.

A stegosaurus's sharp spike surely snapped.

Flying pterodactyl, pretty pterodactyl.

ON THE FUNNY FARM

Knock, knock.
Who's there?
Alpaca.
Alpaca who?
Alpaca the bags. You get the keys.

Knock, knock.
Who's there?
Defence.
Defence who?
Defence is broken and the animals ran away!

Knock, knock.
Who's there?
Chicken.
Chicken who?
Chicken out if you want some company!

Where did the farmer take the animals?

On a field trip.

What did the chicken egg say to the number 8?

"Nice belt!"

What is the smartest animal on the farm?

A mathemachicken.

Why was the chicken arrested?

It was suspected
of fowl play.

Why was the turkey kicked out of
the chicken's baseball game?

For hitting too
many fowl balls.

Why did the chicken cross the road?

TO GET TO THE OTHER SIDE.

Why did the chicken cross the playground?

TO GET TO THE OTHER SLIDE.

Why did the chicken cross the beach?

TO GET TO THE OTHER TIDE.

Why did the hamburger cross the road?

IT WAS FOLLOWING THE CHICKEN.

Why did the french fries cross the road?

THEY WERE FOLLOWING THE HAMBURGER.

Why didn't the tomato cross the road?

IT WAS FOLLOWING THE FRIES, BUT IT COULDN'T KETCHUP.

Why did the chicken cross the road?

THE ROAD HAD IT COMING.

Why did the robot cross the road when it saw a fight?

IT WAS PROGRAMMED BY A CHICKEN.

Why did the elephant cross the road?

IT WAS THE CHICKEN'S DAY OFF.

Why did the chicken go up the stairs?

It had already crossed the road.

How do you grow a vegetarian chicken?

With an eggplant.

Why did the chicken get in trouble?

For using fowl language.

How did the chicken get in the band?

By bringing drumsticks.

Why did the chicken join the gym?

For the eggsercise.

Why did Beethoven get rid of all his chickens?

They kept screaming,
"Bach! Bach! Bach!"

Why do chickens lay eggs?

Because if they dropped
them, they would break.

What does a chicken say when it burps?

"Eggscuse me."

What do evil chickens lay?

Deviled eggs.

What do you call a muddy chicken that
crosses the road and then comes back?

A dirty double-crosser.

Do you know which weekday chickens hate?
Frydays.

How does a chicken tell the time?
One cluck... two cluck... three cluck...

Why did the rooster cross the road?
To impress all the chicks.

What did the cow say to the bull in an argument?
"You're being udderly ridiculous!"

What kind of bull is always sleeping?

A bulldozer.

How do you find a bull that will let you ride it?

Post a want ad on the bulletin board.

Why is it easy to fool a bull calf?

Because it is still gullibull.

Why shouldn't you rip up a drawing of cattle?

Because that is tear-a-bull.

Why did the art teacher tell the student to redo their painting of cattle?

The teacher wanted it to be seen and not herd.

Knock, knock.
Who's there?
Cow says.
Cow says who?
No. Cow says, "Moo."

Knock, knock.
Who's there?
Moo.
Moo who?
Moove it or lose it!

A **legendairy** cow came to the farm to tell **horser** stories. The calf wanted to listen, but its mom said, "No, it's **pasture** bedtime!"

Where do you find most young cows eating?
The calfeteria.

What do you get when you cross a bee with a cow?
Beef!

What did the farmer say to the cow on the roof?

"Get down."

What is a cow's favorite outing?

The mooseum.

Why did the cow cross the road?

To get to the **udder** side!

Why did the cow feel ill at the concert?

Because the band
made moosick.

Why don't cows ever leave the farm?

They hate mooving.

How often do cows get sick?

Once in a blue moon.

What do you get when you cross a cow and a duck?

Milk and quackers!

What kind of cow joins a band?

A moosician.

What do you call a cow who likes scuba diving?

A moorine biologist.

What do you call a cow with no legs?

Ground beef.

What does the cow say every December 25th?

"Mooey Christmas!"

What's every cow's favorite city?

Moo York City.

What is every cow's favorite heavenly body?

The moooon.

Why did the farmer put a bell on the cow?

Its horn didn't work.

Where do you find the most cows in outer space?

On the moon.

What device do cows use in math class?

Cowculators.

Why did the
cow stop singing?

Because it was
really horse.

What do you get from a belly-dancing cow?

A milkshake.

What do you call a cow eating the grass?

A lawn mooer.

What is a cow's favorite drink?

Lemoooonade.

Where do cows go on dates?

The moovie theater!

Why did the cow cancel its date?

It wasn't in the mood to go out.

How do you share a bench with a cow?

Just ask it to moooove over a little.

What do you call a duck that stepped in glue?

A STUCK DUCK.

What do you call a duck that stepped in glue and costs two dollars?

A TWO-BUCK STUCK DUCK.

What do you call a duck that stepped in glue, costs two dollars, and gets hit on the head by an actor?

A STARSTRUCK TWO-BUCK STUCK DUCK!

What do you call a duck that stepped in glue, costs two dollars, gets hit on the head by an actor, and the farmer pulls it free?

LUCKY!

What do you call a duck that gets straight A's?

A wisequacker.

What's a duck's favorite part of the news?

The feather forecast.

What's a duck's favorite ballet?

The Nutquacker.

Why shouldn't you go to a duck doctor?

Most of them are quacks.

What do you call guard ducks on a farm?

Animal quackers.

Why couldn't the duck sell its windows?

They were all quacked.

Why are ducks good at math?

They have their own quackulators.

Who pays for dinner when a duck
and a cow go on a date?

The duck! (It has the bill!)

Which side of a duck has the most feathers?

The outside.

Why did the duck fall apart?

Because there were so many quacks in it!

How does a duck detective catch a bad guy?

He quacks the case.

What did the duck say to the comedian?

**"You really quack
me up!"**

Why is it dangerous to tell a duck jokes?

It might quack up.

Why don't you ask a duck for a quarter?

It only has bills.

What does a duck wear for a fancy black-tie event?

Its duck-xedo.

What is the difference between a duck and a spider?

**A spider has its
feet in a web.
A duck has a
web in its feet.**

Knock, knock.
Who's there?
Foal.
Foal who?
Foal me once, shame on you. Foal me twice, shame on me!

Knock, knock.
Who's there?
Emu.
Emu who?
Are you not emused by these jokes? Please open the door.

Knock, knock.
Who's there?
Goat.
Goat who?
Goat to the door and see for yourself.

Knock, knock.
Who's there?
Goat.
Goat who?
Goat to bed. It's late!

Person 1: "Two goats ate a DVD and a book."
Person 2: "Really? Why did they do that?"
Person 1: "They said they liked the movie, but the book was better."

What did the goat say when its children made a mess?

"You have got to be kidding me!"

What did the goat tell its kids when horses moved in next door?

"Say hay to the new neighbors."

How did Noah encourage the horses to get into the ark?

With rains.

Why can't horses ever agree?

They always say neigh!

How do horses know who's the most popular?

They do a Gallop Poll.

What kind of horse chews with its mouth closed?

**One with good
stable manners.**

Why did the pony get in trouble?

**It wouldn't stop
horsing around.**

The sheep's joke was **baa**ad.
The cow's joke was a**moo**sing.
The pig's joke was **boar**ing.
And the chicken's joke was **egg**cellent!

Why were the ponies kicked out of the theater?

Too much horseplay.

What does finding a horseshoe mean?

There's a barefoot horse somewhere.

What makes a horse feel lousy in spring?

Hay fever.

What did the cow say to the horse?

"Hey, why the long face?"

Why do cowboys ride horses?

They can't carry them.

What did the horse say when it fell over?

"Help! I can't giddyup!"

Why did the pony stop speaking?
It was a little horse.

How is a horse like a storm?

One is reined up. The other rains down.

Where do you take a sick horse?

To the horsepital.

What is a pony's favorite dance?

A barn dance.

What did the llama say when it was going on vacation?

"Alpaca my bag. You-paca my suitcase."

What is a llama's favorite dessert?

A banana spit.

What happens when llama best friends argue?

Llama drama.

What do you call two llamas standing next to a bell?

Llama llama ding dong.

What did the llama say when the sheep bumped into it?

No probllama.

What kind of business did the turtle and llama start together?

A turtleneck sweater store.

Knock, knock.
Who's there?
Three little pigs.
Three little pigs who?
**Three little pigs who are too small
to reach the bell.**

Why do pigs have such pretty houses?
They're great **sty**lists!

Why are pigs great in an emergency?
They love to drive
the hambulance!

What do you call a pig at the
beach who can do magic?
A ham sandwitch!

Where do pigs go when they are sick?

To the **farm**acy to
get some **Oink**ment.

What do you call a pig with no eyes?

Pg.

How do pigs celebrate Valentine's Day?

With hogs and kisses.

What part of a football is like hide-
and-seek on a farm?

The pig's hide.

Why did the farmer teach the pig martial arts?

The farmer wanted
a pork chop.

Why are pigs great comedians?

They're total hams!

What do you call a sheep that was up all night?

A SLEEPY SHEEPY.

What do you call a sheep that was up all night and does ballet?

A LEAPY, SLEEPY SHEEPY.

What do you call a sheep that was up all night, does ballet, and cleans the floors?

A SWEEPY, LEAPY, SLEEPY SHEEPY.

What do you call a sheep that was up all night, does ballet, cleans the floors, and hates spending money?

A CHEAPY, SWEEPY, LEAPY, SLEEPY SHEEPY.

What do you call a sheep that was up all night, does ballet, cleans the floors, hates spending money, and is at the top of a mountain?

A STEEPY, CHEAPY, SWEEPY, LEAPY, SLEEPY SHEEPY.

What do you call a sheep that was up all night, does ballet, cleans the floors, hates spending money, is at the top of a mountain, and is ready for bed?

TIRED!

Which animal's paintings hang in the
Metropolitan Museum of Art?

Pablo Pigcasso.

What did the farmer say to the sheep on the roof?

"Baa!" (Sheep don't
understand English.)

Where do sheep get their hair cut?

At the baa-baa shop.

Why do sheep like to dance?

They are good
at baallet!

Why did the person shove a
sheep into the computer?

They wanted more ram.

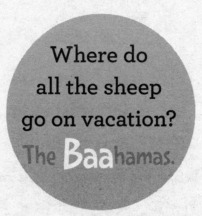

Where do all the sheep go on vacation? The Baahamas.

Why did the farmer try to get his lamb onto a rocket?

The farmer had always wanted a spacesheep.

How do you mail a turkey?

Bird class.

Why wouldn't they let the turkey into the buffet?

Because it would gobble up the food.

Why did the turkey get cut from its baseball team?

Too many fowl balls.

Why was the turkey in time-out?

It used fowl language.

What does a limping turkey sound like?

Wobble, wobble, wobble.

"Let's take a trip," the farmer said.
"I'm **woolly, woolly** excited!" said the sheep.
"Sounds **boar**ing," moaned the pig.
"**Neigh**," said the horse.
And the cow just wouldn't **moo**ve.

What does a donkey do when you tell him a joke?
He haws.

What do donkeys say at Christmas?
Mule-tide greetings!

What does a donkey say when it likes something?
"Hee-haw-some!"

What country has the most donkeys?
Bray-sil.

Why did the donkey join a band?
It wanted to bray some tunes.

Can you say these tongue twisters?

The unlucky duck got stuck in a yucky truck.

The remorseful horse was forced to reverse its course.

The sleepy sheep slowly slipped to sleep.

Cranky cows vow to plough with a scowl.

The angry ram raged around the rambling range.

The sunbathing sheep suffered severe sunstroke.

Pink pigs tickle purple turtles.

Childish children chase chunky chickens.

Gloating goats slowly row green rowboats.

TOADILY TERRIFIC REPTILES AND AMPHIBIANS

What are an alligator's favorite shoes?

Crocs!

What do you call an alligator detective?

An investigator.

What is a cobra's favorite clothing item?

A hoodie.

Why shouldn't you let a crocodile tell you a story?

Because their tales
are so long!

How did the person know how many
reptiles were in the area?

They checked
the crocodial!

What do reptiles use to tell time?

A clockodile!

What game does a chameleon always win?

Hide-and-seek.

What is the chameleon's favorite book?

The Lizard of Oz.

What did the chameleon's mom say
on the first day of school?

"Don't worry, you'll blend right in."

What is the funniest lizard?

The stand-up chameleon.

Never let a bearded dragon tell you a story. It will drag on and on and on!

I think I have a lot of chameleons, but I'm not sure . . .

Knock, knock.
Who's there?
Frog.
Frog who?
Frogotten who I am already?

What is a frog's favorite fast food?
French flies!

Why is the frog always in a good mood?
It eats whatever bugs it.

What's a frog's favorite sport?
Croaket.

What is a frog's favorite drink?

Croak-a-cola.

What is a frog's favorite pie?

Croakonut cream.

What is a frog's favorite forest friend?

The ribbit.

A man went to the doctor.
"How can I help?" the doctor asked.
The man said, "I think I'm a frog."
"Well, I'm sorry," replied the doctor, "but I
think you're going to croak!"

What do you call a frog that loves exercise?

A JOGGY FROGGY.

What do you call a frog that loves exercise and is wearing a toupee?

A WIGGY, JOGGY FROGGY.

What do you call a frog that loves exercise, is wearing a toupee, and has a stick in its mouth?

A TWIGGY, WIGGY, JOGGY FROGGY.

What do you call a frog that loves exercise, is wearing a toupee, has a stick in its mouth, and barks?

ROVER!

Do you think princes like frogs?

Toadally.

Do you want to know how many different kinds of frogs are in the pond?

No, just give me the toad-al.

Why couldn't the frog find its car?

It had been toad.

What's the only kind of shoes frogs will wear?

Open-toad sandals.

Knock, knock.
Who's there?
Newt.
Newt who?
Newt to town. Wanna hang out?

Why were there lizards all over the bathroom wall?
They're reptiles.

Who is a lizard's favorite scientist?
Isaac Newton!

What did the lizard say on its first day of school?

"I'm newt!"

What do you call thousands of white lizards falling from the sky?

A blizard.

What do you call a rhyming lizard?

A raptile.

Why did the skink fail its creative writing assignment?

It lost its tale!

Person 1: "What is a poisonous snake's biggest fear?"
Person 2: "I don't know. What?"
Person 1: "Biting its own tongue."

What did the hyena say to the snake?

"You're hissterical!"

Why are snakes terrible friends?

They're always throwing a hissy fit!

Why did the person shove a snake into the computer?

It needed more bytes!

What is the sweetest snake?

The piethon!

What do you call a snake with a migraine?

AN ACHY SNAKEY.

What do you call a snake with a migraine that loves to cook?

A BAKEY, ACHY SNAKEY.

What do you call a snake with a migraine that loves to cook and whose alarm is going off?

A WIDE-AWAKEY, BAKEY, ACHY SNAKEY.

What do you call a snake with a migraine that loves to cook, whose alarm is going off, and that tells lies?

A FAKEY, WIDE-AWAKEY, BAKEY, ACHY SNAKEY.

What do you call a snake with a migraine that loves to cook, whose alarm is going off, that tells lies, and is on the road?

SQUISHED!

Which cartoon character is a snake's favorite?

Venom.

What do you call a snake on a jobsite wearing a hard hat?

A boa constructor.

What do you get when you combine a snake and a snowman?

Frostbite.

Why did the snake quit the movie business?

There were no parts it could really sink its teeth into.

Why is it impossible to fool a snake?

You can't pull its leg.

What school subject do snakes like the most?

Hisstory.

How do you check if a snake is a baby?
See if it has a rattle.

Why do kids love snakes?
Because they are fangtastic.

A snake slithered right through a blizzard
To see the world's greatest wise wizard.
It hated to slide
And wanted to stride,
With legs that would make it a lizard!

Snakes lie on scales, but cats lie on **fur**niture.

Snakes have big fangs, but they're completely armless!

The snake wanted to make a good point, but it didn't have a leg to stand on.

Knock, knock.

Who's there?

Fangs.

Fangs who?

Fangs for inviting me over!

Knock, knock.

Who's there?

Toad.

Toad who?

Toad my car. Now I have to walk.

Knock, knock.

Who's there?

Toad.

Toad who?

Toadally love this joke!

A cat might have nine lives, but
which animal has more?

**The toad. It croaks
every night.**

What is a good snack for a toad?

French flies and a diet croak.

Where do turtles stop on road trips?

The Shell station.

Where can a turtle get a new tail?

A retail store.

Lawyer: Did you steal that food?
Tortoise: Turtley!

A turtle didn't know what to do;
There was a party it had to get to.
It was two miles away
And took three years and a day
Till it said, "Happy birthday to you!"

Can you say these tongue twisters?

The fifth frog's floppy feet flipped.

Shaky snakes shyly slither in silence.

Snakes slither through thick, thorny thistles.

The seventh thirsty snake slithered silently.

The lazy lizard licked lemon lollipops.

Slippery snakes scare skittish sheep.

The greedy green gecko gobbled grass.

Three fine frogs threw free throws.

The vile crocodile cracked a creepy smile.

SHELLEBRATE SEA LIFE

How do dolphins resolve their differences?

They just flipper coin.

How do you give a dolphin directions?

However you'd like, but be sure you're Pacific.

What did the dolphin do when it got angry?

It flipped out.

Why do dolphins make so few mistakes?

Because almost everything they do is on porpoise.

Judge: How do you plead?
Dolphin: I'm innocent!
Squid: It did it on porpoise!

Why couldn't the baby beluga hear its mom?

It was whale-ing!

What do clams call a party?

A shellebration.

Person 1: "I'm mad at all the clams."
Person 2: "Really? Why?"
Person 1: "They're being shellfish!"

What do you call a crab that won't share?

A GRABBY CRABBY.

What do you call a crab that won't share and drives you places?

A CABBY, GRABBY CRABBY.

What do you call a crab that won't share, drives you places, and pokes your foot?

A JABBY, CABBY, GRABBY CRABBY.

What do you call a crab that won't share, drives you places, pokes your foot, and does cool dance moves?

A DABBY, JABBY, CABBY, GRABBY CRABBY.

What do you call a crab that won't share, drives you places, pokes your foot, does cool dance moves, and gets chased by a seagull?

LUNCH!

Knock, knock.
Who's there?
I'm in the orca.
I'm in the orca who?
I'm in the orcastra, and I play bass.

Knock, knock.
Who's there?
Cod.
Cod who?
Cod you let me in, please?

Knock, knock.
Who's there?
Fin.
Fin who?
Fintastic to see you!

Knock, knock.
Who's there?
I'm a fish.
I'm a fish who?
I'm a fish-ially here!

Why were the fish upset with the electric eels?

**The eels' behavior
was shocking!**

What country probably has the most fish?

Finland.

What do you call a bunch of fish in perfect harmony?

Coral singers.

What do librarians do when they
want to catch smart fish?

They use bookworms.

Why don't fish play tennis?

They're afraid of the net.

Why do fish have trouble in school?

Because all their work is below C-level.

What did the magician fish say?

"Pick a cod, any cod."

What do you call a tuna fish with human legs?

A two-knee fish.

How do you get in touch with a fish?

Just drop it a line.

How do fish get to school?

An octu-bus.

What is a fish's favorite hobby?

Coral-aoke.

A racing fish sped through the ocean,
Got thirsty, and drank a strange potion.
When it finished the drink,
It started to sink
And now only swims in slow motion.

What do you get when you cross a small fish with a young dog?

A puppy guppy.

Where do fish sleep at night?

In their waterbeds.

Where do all the sick fish go?

The emergensea room.

Why did the student put a fish on their piano?

So they could learn music scales.

Why was the fish so smart? It spent its whole life in a **school.**

What do you get when you cross a fish and an elephant?
Swim trunks.

What do you call a fish with no eyes?
Fsh.

What is the most musical part of a fish?
The scales.

Fish love Sunday, but they hate **Fry**day!

Why was the fish at the bottom of the ocean?

It dropped out of school.

What is the difference between a guitar and a fish?

You can't tuna fish.

What made the fish blush?

It could see the lake's **bottom.**

Why are shellfish the worst friends?

They're always crabby!

Why did the detective quiz the shellfish?

He thought something looked fishy.

How did the shellfish frustrate the detective?

They all clammed up.

Knock, knock.
Who's there?
Great white shark eat.
Great white shark eat who?
Great white shark eat *you*!

Who did the shellfish use for protection?

The mussels.

Where do shellfish go to borrow money fast?

The prawnbroker.

What are the tastiest underwater animals?

Octopies.

What do you call a surgeon with eight arms?

A doctopus.

How many tickles does it take to
make an octopus laugh?

Ten-tickles.

Why don't the crab and the lobster
share the ocean well?

Because they're both
really shellfish.

What game do salmon love to play?

Go Fish.

What is the most popular game at the fish party?

Salmon Says.

How are sharks like computers?

They both have
mega bites!

There once was an angry young shark
That saw a dog down at the park.
It flashed a big grin
And said, "Doggy, get in.
My bite is much worse than my bark!"

What type of shark helps you see?
A great light shark.

What type of shark loves Halloween?

The great fright shark.

What did the shark use to cook a stir-fry?

A woktopus.

How do you catch an unusual baby shark?

Unique up on it.

Why do baby sharks swim in saltwater?

Because pepper water makes them sneeze!

What is a shark's favorite game show?

Whale of Fortune.

Why can't you trust a shark?

They tell great white lies.

What kind of shark is good at building?

A hammerhead.

Where do sharks go on vacation?

Finland.

Why did all the seals leave the United Kingdom?

They were afraid of Wales.

Why did the squid win the art contest?

Its ink drawing made a splash!

What do sharks like on their peanut butter sandwich?

Lots of **jelly**fish.

Someone robbed the underwater bank. No one could find the thief until the squid cracked the case. "How did you know who did it?" asked the judge. "I just had an *ink*ling," said the squid.

Why didn't the squid ever invite anyone over for dinner?

Because it lived on the ocean's bottom.

What underwater creature do you put on your feet?

A **sock**topus.

What underwater creature should you never touch?

A shocktopus.

What underwater creature tells the best jokes?

A knock-knock-topus!

What underwater creature is best at sports?

A jocktopus.

What has eight legs and super-sharp teeth?

A croctopus.

What did the dolphin say to the sad whale?

What are you blubbering about?

Why are whales fierce pirates?

They make you walk the plankton.

Why was the train station at the beach so big?

It needed room for the whale-way tracks.

"**Do you know where you can weigh a whale?**"
"No. Where?"
"**At the whale-weigh station.**"

Whales love listening to the orcastra, but the insect band really bugs them.

What do you do when you're swallowed by a whale?

Start running and don't stop until you're all pooped out.

Why do whales drink orange juice?

For the vitamin sea.

Did you know whales can squirt ink when they're scared?

Nah, just squidding!

A whale swam by, learning to sing.
In water its singing would ring.
But when it would croon,
It sang out of tune.
You never have heard a worse thing!

Where did the whale store its makeup?

In its octopurse.

Where do all the sick whales go?

Straight to the sturgeon.

What do whales chew on?

Blubber gum.

The dolphin told a bad joke on **porpoise**, the orca told a **killer** joke, and the fish's joke **floundered**, but the shark's joke was **jawsome**!

Can you say these tongue twisters?

Can clammy clams cram into cans?

A shiny seal will squeal for an appealing meal.

Selfish fish sell shellfish shells.

Sally the silly starfish sat on a seahorse.

The porpoise pluckily played pool.

The whale winked wryly at the ray.

Which whale whined while winning?

An orca named Anita ate orchards of apples.

Flying fish flee from a free fish-fry.

YOU CAN WRITE JOKES TOO!

Are you ready to create your own jokes that are silly, punny, and so HIGH-larious that your comedy career will blast off?

Follow these tips to write your very own jokes. Once you have a collection of jokes you like, perform them for your family or make a joke book of your own.

Find the Funny

What makes you laugh? Make a list of things you find funny: How your dog looks when she's covered in bubbles in the bath. The time your grandma sent your little sister the toy *you'd* been wanting for *her* birthday. The way gelatin jiggles. The flamingos at the zoo standing on one leg. So wacky! If you start with a situation or image that makes you laugh, chances are that others will think it's funny too.

What do you call a dog in the bath?
A sham**poodle.**

Why does a flamingo stand on one leg?
Because if he lifted the other leg. he'd fall.

Sneak in a Surprise

A good joke sets the audience's expectations and then—*Twist!*—takes the topic in a new, surprising direction.

What time is it when ten elephants run past you?

Ten past one!

What has fur, whiskers, a tail, ears like a cat, and meows like a cat, but is not a cat?

A kitten.

Exaggerate

Use words with BIG meaning, then twist that meaning. Snails are known for being v-e-e-e-r-r-r-y slow. So if you call a snail fast, what does that mean?

What did the speedy snail say before he crossed the sidewalk to join his friends?

See you on Tuesday.

Compare and Contrast

Find a surprising similarity between things that are otherwise very different.

What did the chicken egg say to the number 8?

Nice belt!

Why did the goose get pulled over on the highway?

It was honking at everyone.

Create puns

A pun is a joke that plays on two meanings of the same word or two words that sound the same. Experiment with the meaning and sounds of words to write "punny" jokes.

Lots of words have a few different meanings: *charge* can mean filling a battery with electricity or it can mean an animal running into something.

Why did the girl tie a cord to the rhino?

She thought it would be good at charging her phone!

Bare, meaning "without covering," and *bear*, the animal, sound the same.

Why did the grizzly go to the shoe store?

She was tired of bear feet.

Lots of jokes play on the similar sounds of words.

Knock knock!
Who's there?
Goat.
Goat who?
Goat to the door and see for yourself.

You can also create a pun by separating the parts of a word. Most words have other words inside them or parts of the word sound similar to another word.

Which dinosaur was the most polite?
The **please**iosaur.

Start at the end

Write the punchline—the funny ending of the joke—first. Then come up with a question that the punchline answers.

Think of a word or common phrase. Does it sound similar to any other words? Does it have a sound-alike word that you can switch out?

What do wild animals sing on your birthday?

Hippo bird-day to you!

Why did my mom give my dad a dog and a watch?

She heard he was having a **ruff** time.

Ask a Question

Many jokes start with a question. The punchline is a funny spin on the real answer, a pun, or other silly surprise. You can use basic question starters to write some pretty terrific jokes.

"What did the ___ say to the ___?"

What did the flea say to the mouse?

"You're enormouse!"

What did the bunny say to the carrot?

It's been nice
gnawing you!

"How many ___ does it take to ___?"

How many tickles does it take to
make an octopus laugh?

Ten-tickles.

Get out a notepad or device and try these tips. Don't worry if your jokes aren't funny at first. Keep practicing and you'll be a clever comedian soon enough.

Now get quacking up!